In a land far awa... Pearl and Peter. They love their home even though it is one of the coldest places on earth. You see, they are penguins and they stay very warm. Their feathers have oil on them to protect them from the frigid temperatures here. One day Pearl turned to Peter and said, "I think it's time we added to our family, don't you think, Peter?" Peter agreed and they began to gather twigs and stones to build a nest. Pearl would have liked a big family but penguins only lay one egg. "Isn't it the prettiest light green color?" she asked. Peter said, "I would love it even if it were purple, Pearl. Where are you going to put it?" "I keep it in a flap of skin next to my stomach," she replied, "Our little one will be nice and warm there!"

When Pearl had to leave the nest to eat, she would pass the egg to Peter by juggling it from her feet to his feet. Peter then kept the egg in his pocket. In this way the egg never touches the ground and stays warm.

One day Peter exclaimed, "I hear something cracking, Pearl! Oh, my, here it comes!" The egg did indeed crack open and out popped the cutest little chick. Peter asked, "What shall we name her?" "Why we will name her after my great grandmother Penelope." Pearl said. "Oh, no we won't," Peter retorted, "That name is just too long." Pearl began to cry and Peter had to think quickly. "Don't cry, my dear, Penelope she'll be. But can we call her Penny for short?" Pearl smiled up at him through her tears and said, "OK, that is a nice nickname."

Peter and Pearl were very happy. Penny grew quickly and soon the family could go fishing together. But their favorite thing to do was sliding down icebergs. "Weeeeeeee!" cried Penny as she would slide faster and faster until she plopped into the water.

One day while sliding on her back, Penny looked up and saw some seagulls flying overhead. They looked like they were having such fun. Penny wanted to be up there with them. She waddled as fast as she could and jumped into the air. She flapped her little wings and...KERPLOP! Penny fell right to the ground. Pearl and Peter laughed and laughed. "Oh, Penny, that was so cute!" they exclaimed. But Penny had the most hurt look on her face. "I want to fly just like those seagulls," she cried. Pearl and Peter looked at one another, not knowing how to tell her the bad news. Finally, Peter spoke, "Don't get any silly ideas, Penny. Penguins can't fly. We lost that ability millions of years ago. Now our wings are just small flippers to help us swim." Penny looked at her arms and then up at the seagulls' big wings. She didn't say anything, but she knew in her heart that someday she was going to fly like a real bird. When Penny made that promise to herself, she did not know it would take her on many adventures to faraway places.

PENNY'S FIRST ADVENTURE

Penny loved life within the penguin colony. Every day seemed to melt into the next day, yet Penny was learning something new all the time. "Mom! Dad! Watch me dive down and catch these red krill!" cried Penny. Bright red krill look like tiny shrimp and are what penguin's love to eat most.

"We're watching, Penny. But you be careful. You know we must watch out for the seals," warned

Pearl. Seals and killer whales like to have a penguin for their dinner.

As Pearl and Peter watched, Penny began her clumsy waddle and slid down the ice into the sea. Already Penny was a good swimmer, catching her snack with great ease. Whoosh, whoosh…went the water as Penny glided through it. Pearl and Peter could see Penny the entire time she was under water. It is so clean and clear in the Antarctic. Some penguins have been known to stay underwater as long as one minute and swim as fast as twenty miles per hour.

Soon Penny grew tired and she flopped onto the ice. "Whew! That was fun!! She said. The family snuggled together watching the sun as it completed a circle in the sky. Since Antarctica has all daylight for five months of the year, the sun does not rise or set. It only circles the sky. How would a penguin know it is time to sleep? When it is tired!

Off in the distance there was the sound of an airplane engine. Who was coming to invade the land of ice and snow?

The next morning Peter awakened with a start. Something was different. "Look over there, Pearl," Peter said as he pointed. "Those things are awfully tall, even for Emperor penguins." Emperor penguins are the largest penguins of all, with some being three and one half feet tall. Pearl looked and sure enough, there were some big dark figures coming toward the penguin colony. Pearl began to speak, "Maybe those creatures are 'humans'. My friend Patty told me about them. They carry little boxes that they look through and then press a button. The boxes even make a little buzzing noise. Their fur looks funny and every one of them is a different color. Ha! Too bad they don't walk as well as we do."

What they saw was a tourist group that had chartered a plane in Australia for a visit to Antarctica. While there they would use their cameras to take pictures of the wildlife. "Oh, Bob, aren't these penguins just darling? Why, they look like little fat men dressed in tuxedos. Honey, look at that cute baby over there," said the woman as she pointed to Penny.

Penny showed little interest in the people. She wanted to look at the huge bird from which the people came. Why, it had flown just like those seagulls. But it made so much noise! "How can it fly with a hole in its side?" Penny wondered. Since penguins can only see what is close to them, she waddled closer and closer to the airplane. Soon she was right by the cargo door.

"As long as I've come this far, I might as well have a look inside," thought Penny. "Maybe I'll find a clue that will help me learn to fly." And with that idea she jumped inside.

"Oh, oh, it's dark in here," whispered Penny. She almost turned back but her curiosity got the best of her. She wandered around many crates and boxes in the cargo hold. All of a sudden Penny heard footsteps. Wham! The cargo door slammed shut and she could not even see her flipper in front of her face. Penny shrieked with fear, "Help! Let me out! Mom, Dad, help me!"

Outside, two men prepared the plane for takeoff. One of them asked, "Fred, did you hear something? It sounded like 'ark, ark, ark' to me. Shall we have a look inside, mate?" "Naw, Dennis, I didn't hear a sound. The only thing it could be is those boxes creaking from this bloody cold weather. Let's get out of here." The other man answered.

Even though Penny kept wailing, her shrieks were soon drowned out by the plane's loud engines. Soon the plane began to move faster and faster. Just as its skis lifted off the ice, Penny fell backwards. Crack! Her head hit one of the boxes. She was knocked out and fell to the floor of the plane. Penny was missing her first flight!

PENNY'S SECOND ADVENTURE

Penny blinked her eyes as she slowly awakened. It was so dark she thought she must still have her eyes shut. Then she remembered what happened. She had been looking inside this big bird and now she was trapped.

"Oh, my, it's so noisy," Penny thought as she stood up, "and I feel so dizzy." Why, she could barely stand. Then she thought of how the big bird had dropped from the sky. "Could I be in the air now?"

wondered Penny. She no sooner had that idea, as she suddenly fell down and began to slide forward.

A few of the boxes were sliding with her. She bumped her head again, but it was nothing compared to the bumps that followed. BUMP! BUMP! BUMPETY, BUMP, BUMP! Penny was afraid now. It sounded like the end of the world.

Up in the cockpit the co-pilot said to the pilot, "That was a really smooth landing, Captain. It will be nice to see a bit of Wellington." Wellington is the capital city of a country called New Zealand.

As the plane coasted to a stop, Penny felt as if the world might not end after all. She heard a noise that was not as loud as the plane's engine. It was the unloading ramp coming up to the cargo hold door.

"Oh! My eyes hurt!" cried Penny, as light flooded into the hold. "I'll have to make a break for it now or I'll be stuck in this big bird forever." As soon as the door was open, out hopped Penny. The belt on the ramp began moving and Penny was on it!

"Hey, John! Look at this!" one of the workers yelled as he pointed at Penny. "Catch it or we will be in big trouble!" cried John. But just then an alarm sounded and both men looked away. Penny jumped off the ramp and waddled toward a building. "I know I saw some Emperor penguins over here," Penny said. "Maybe they can help me find Mom and Dad." Penny hurried over to the group of black and white figures, but they were NOT Emperor penguins. It was a group of men dressed in tuxedos. "Oh no, not more humans!" wailed Penny.

In her panic, she ran to some women standing nearby. Whoosh! A sudden gust of wind blew one of their long skirts right over Penny. She was now hidden! "Hey! Has anyone here seen a penguin?" a man asked. "Now what would a penguin be doing here, you silly man?" asked one of the women. "We don't know, but we had better find it. Sorry to bother you. Good boy." The man answered. The woman who had spoken looked angry. "Good boy? Can't he see that we are all women? What's the matter with him?" Another woman, who was very clever, figured out the mistake. "I think he was saying good-bye, but with his Australian accent you thought it was good boy. Ha! Ha!"

Meanwhile Penny, still under the skirt, had a plan. "If only I can stay with this group, I might escape. I just hope I don't get stepped on." A van had come and all the women got into it. Penny hopped in, too, and hid under a seat in the back. "Where to, ladies?" asked the driver. "We've always wanted to see the Waitomo Caves," one said.

Then one of the women decided to have a snack. She took out a can of sardines and opened it. Just then the van hit a bump and the sardines spilled onto the floor. Penny had been so afraid that she had not even thought about food...until now. "Fish! Yummy!" she cried as she crawled to the sardines. Penny ate them all and went back under the seat. The woman who had spilled them kept looking for the sardines, but they were nowhere to be found. "It's a miracle that they do not smell. Where did they go?" she wondered.

Penny could not help herself. She burst out laughing, as she was the only one who knew where the sardines were. "What was that noise?" a woman asked. "I think the van squeaked when we went over that bump," another said. "Whew!" thought Penny, "That was a close. I better keep my big beak shut.

Soon the van came to a stop. "We are here, ladies," said the driver. They all got out of the van. Penny waited a few minutes. Then she hopped out, too. "Where am I?" Penny wondered.

Penny heard a scream. She saw two of the ladies helping another one to walk. "Oh, Louise, can't you do anything right? Now we will have to take you to the doctor. That means we cannot see the caves today." Penny watched as the people got back into the van and drove away. She looked at the dark hole in the ground ahead. "I think I'll have a look in there," she thought. Then she stopped and remembered the last time she had this thought. "Certainly, I won't get trapped this time. One look won't hurt. And I see a light."

Penny went into the cave. She felt a rush of cold air. Then it seemed as if she were in a wide, open space. There were little lights everywhere! "Are these stars twinkling?" asked Penny, her eyes full of wonder.

The lights answered her! "We are the glowworms of Waitomo Caves," millions of tiny voices said. "Many people come to see us from all over the world. What kind of person are you?" Penny laughed. "I am not a human. I am a penguin. "A penguin! What are you doing here?" asked the glowworms. "It's a long story," said Penny. "You see, penguins cannot fly. I thought this big bird could help me learn to fly, but I was lucky to escape from it. What am I going to do now?"

"We know someone just like you," said the glowworms. Penny got excited and asked, "Who? Who? Another penguin is here, too?" "No, he's not a penguin. You'll find him in the woods outside the caves. He looks like a ball. Just call 'Keewee, Keewee'. Good luck to you." The glowworms replied.

Penny went out of the cave and waddled toward the woods. Sure enough, there was a ball near a tree. "Keewee! Keewee!" Penny called. The ball came to life and began to run away. Penny had found a kiwi bird. Kiwi birds cannot fly either. They are very shy and that is why this one was running away. "Wait! Wait! Please don't leave me!" yelled Penny. The bird turned and watched Penny who was beginning to cry.

"Aw, stop those tears," it said. "What is the matter with you?" "I'm lost and I can't fly," sniffed Penny. "Well, I can help you with the first part, but I can't fly either. By the by, my name is Kelly and I am a kiwi bird. Who are you?"

"I'm Penny the penguin. Can you really help me?" she asked. "Sure enough, mate. Where do you want to go to?" asked Kelly. "Right now, I'd like to get on one of those birds and go home," said Penny.

Kelly thought for a minute. "That's easy enough. All you have to do is hide behind a rock. When one of those vans comes, just jump on it. They are always bringing people here. Then when it stops at the airport, just jump off."

"OK, but can I ask you one question before I leave, Kelly?" "Sure, ask ahead," he said. "Kelly, have you ever wanted to fly?" Kelly looked at Penny as if she were crazy. "Not on your life, Penny. I have enough trouble trying to find worms and insects to eat. I like it here on the ground. That flying stuff is for the birds!" "But you are a bird, Kelly," said Penny. "Hurrumph! Never wanted to fly and I never will," he replied. "Well, I want to fly and I shall...someday.

Thank you for your help." Penny waved good-bye with her flipper.

Penny went back to the cave's opening and hid just like Kelly had said. "Glow-be, glow-bye, Penny," chimed the glowworms as they saw Penny hurry past. "Glow-luck, glow-luck."

Penny found an empty van and jumped onto it. It was dark when the van got to the airport. "No one will be able to see me now," thought Penny. "I sure hope I pick the right bird. I can't wait to see Mom and Dad." Penny hopped into the nearest airplane with an open door. On its side was painted—Qantas Airways. Where is Penny going now?

PENNY'S THIRD ADVENTURE

This airplane did not scare Penny nearly as much as the first one had. She leaned against a box to brace herself for the landing.

"Home already? This trip was a lot shorter than the first bird I rode. Maybe this one could fly much faster," thought Penny, "I sure wish I knew the secret of flight. I will find out, but first I will visit Mom and Dad."

After the door opened, Penny rushed over to get a good look at home. Where was all the ice and snow? "Oh, no!" wailed Penny, "Where am I?" Penny was in shock and did not see the net being thrown over her head. "AARK! AARK! Let me go!" cried Penny as the man scooped her up into the air. "I've got you now, you little devil. You can wriggle all you want, but you won't get out of this," said the man.

"What have you got there, mate?" asked another man. "Some silly looking bird. Thought I might take it home and the wife could make a soup with it," the first man said. "Don't know if I'd bother...looks too thin to me. Better give it to the animal authorities. They'll know what to do with it," said the other. "OK, I'll take it there right now," replied the man holding the net. And with that, he walked under an arch that said – WELCOME TO MELBOURNE.

"What have you got there?" asked Mr. Strafford, the head of animal regulations. "Looks almost like a penguin." As the man removed the net from Penny, she collapsed onto the floor. She was very weak from struggling in the net. "What are you going to do with it?" asked Penny's captor. "I will call my friend, a zoologist," answered Mr. Strafford. He got on the "telly". (That's what they used to call the telephone in Australia in the olden days.) He spoke for a few minutes and listened for quite a few more. Then looking quite satisfied, he rang off saying, "Thanks, you old bloke. I knew you would have the best plan."

Mr. Strafford came from behind his desk and walked toward Penny. "First thing, little one, we are going to get you some food," he said. "Then you are going to meet some distant cousins of yours."

Penny eyed the man wearily, watching him leave the room. She was too weak to even think of escaping. As a matter of fact, she wasn't even afraid anymore. The man came back and set a pan of water and a dish near Penny. He picked Penny up and put her beak near the dish. "I brought you some whale food, little one. We happened to have a shipment going out with a boat. Come on, eat some," coaxed the man.

Penny smelled something familiar. "Krill? Can this be my favorite food?" wondered Penny. And with that thought, she began to eat, slowly at first. Then after a long drink of water, she gobbled up the rest. "My oh my! You must have been hungry!" exclaimed the nice man. Penny felt very tired now. Soon her eyes closed and she was fast asleep.

In the meantime, Mr. Strafford had brought a woman in to see Penny. The lady was an animal doctor called a veterinarian. "Well, Dr. Val, think that little bird will make it?" he asked. Dr. Val examined Penny closely and said, "It looks quite healthy to me.

I hope you didn't feed it too much." "Only as much as I would have eaten," he said. "That's what I was afraid of," Dr. Val laughed as she patted Mr. Strafford's belly. "You'll soon have to waddle like a penguin yourself." He chuckled and asked, "So, Dr. Val, what are you going to do with your bird?" "My bird!" she exclaimed. "Well, I have two choices. First, I could keep her as a pet. But then my home would smell like fish all the time. Second, I could take her to the zookeeper. But I hate seeing animals in cages. Wait! I know! I'll take her to Phillip Island and she can join the fairy penguins there!" Dr. Val bent down and picked up Penny who was still asleep.

When Penny opened her eyes, she thought she must be dreaming. A wave had rolled up onto the shore and hundreds of penguins were everywhere! They waddled quickly across the beach. "Wait! Wait for me!" yelled Penny as she ran after the closest group. The other penguins looked back at Penny and one began to scream, "Run! Run! There's a giant after us! " Penny turned around, but she couldn't see a giant anywhere. Then she understood. <u>She</u> was the giant. These penguins of Phillip Island were so small that Penny seemed as though she was on stilts.

The thought of herself on stilts made Penny laugh so hard she could not run. The other penguins heard her laughing and stopped running too. "What's so funny?" they demanded. Even these penguins were a curious bunch.

"You are all so short," explained Penny. "You are the ones who stick out like a sore flipper," replied one penguin who seemed to be the leader. "I'm sorry. I didn't mean to insult you. My name is Penny. What kind of penguins are you?" she asked.

"We are the blue penguins of Phillip Island. The people here call us fairy penguins. They come here every night to watch our parade," he said. "You have a parade every night?" asked Penny. "No, but these silly humans think we do. We just come ashore and walk to our burrows. They love to watch us and take our pictures," the leader replied.

"Let's really give them something to take a picture of. I am going to fly today," Penny said. "You are crazy, Penny. No penguin can fly," the group said. "I am going to," said Penny, "I have it all figured out. First, we need to build a ramp."

All the fairy penguins helped. Before too long, Penny had herself a nice ramp. "How will you fly, Penny?" asked one of the fairy penguins. "I will run as fast as I can up this ramp. When I get to the top, I will jump and flap my flippers as hard as I can. Then I am going to fly home. It was nice meeting you all and thank you for helping me to reach my goal of flying," Penny said as she bid them farewell. The fairy penguins were not so sure that Penny could stay in the air very long.

To make for a nice soft landing, they had placed the ramp near the water. They watched as Penny took a deep breath. She waddled very fast to the top of the ramp. All the penguins were cheering wildly. At the top of the ramp, Penny took another deep breath and jumped.

"I'm flying! I'm flying!" she cried as she flapped her "wings". KERSPLASH! Penny hit the water in a belly flop. "Oh, well, back to the drawing board," thought Penny. She was so disappointed she did not see the net she was swimming toward. Soon her feet and flippers were all tangled up. "Oh, no! Not again! I'm caught! Help! Help!" she screamed.

Soon the net was lifted from the water and Penny found herself on the deck of a large boat. She looked back and could barely see Phillip Island. She was sad to be leaving the fairy penguins, but maybe this boat would take her home to Mom and Dad. How she missed them!

Penny would spend many days and nights on this boat. Had she been able to read, she would have seen the letters GOOD HOPE painted on its side. At least Penny had plenty to eat. When the nets were brought in, she was able to sneak out and grab a few fish. As the days wore on, Penny began to wonder when she would see land again.

PENNY'S FOURTH ADVENTURE

Penny did not enjoy life on the big boat as she was so lonely. At least she had plenty of fish to eat, but she still missed her favorite food – krill. She also had to be very careful to stay out of sight whenever humans were around.

"I am not going to get caught again, even though Mr. Strafford in Australia was rather nice," Penny vowed. She wondered when the boat would reach her home in Antarctica. Penny was a bit worried, because the air felt as though it was getting warmer instead of colder. In fact, Penny was feeling quite warm herself. Soon she yawned, closed her eyes, and was asleep in no time.

Penny heard noises and realized it was shouts from the crew. "There is the Cape! What a sight for sore eyes, eh, mate?" one of the crew said. "We will set Capetown on fire tonight! It will be a jolly good time!" another man replied.

Penny had heard the word "fire" before. One of the planes was refueling at the airport, when a man had dropped a stick from his mouth. Soon flames had been everywhere. People began screaming and ran away. It had not looked like a "jolly good time" to her.

Penny decided she would have to jump ship before it got to this place called Capetown. A fire was one thing she wanted to miss!

As the ship was coming into port, Penny leaned over the side. If only there had been an iceberg to slide down, it would have been perfect. "It feels so good to be gliding through the water again," thought Penny happily.

When Penny surfaced, she knew what she saw must be a mirage. She was near an island! On its shore was a large colony of penguins! Penny scrambled up onto the beach to meet her distant relatives. Unlike Penny, these penguins had a black stripe on their chest and some white on their faces.

"Where am I?" asked Penny, "And who are you?" One of the penguins stepped forward and spoke, "We are the penguins of Dyer Island, near the Cape of Good Hope." Penny looked crestfallen as she said, "It was my good hope that I was home, but this is not Antarctica, is it?" The penguins shook their heads. "You are near the southern tip of Africa, Penny. Do you know where that is?" Now it was Penny's turn to shake her head. One of the penguins began to draw a map in the sand. "Here is where you came from, Penny, and here is where you are now," it explained. "Oh, no!" whined Penny, "I'm even farther from home than I was before!

Penny turned and walked away from the colony so they would not see her tears. She stopped in her tracks suddenly! She slowly turned around and said, "I never told you my name. How did you know it?"

One of the group called a "spokes-penguin", said, "We have been waiting for you for quite some time, Penny. You see, the Wise One told us all about you." Penny looked thoughtful as she asked, "The Wise One? Who is that" "He is the oldest and smartest of all the penguins on Dyer Island. He can even foresee future events!"

Penny did not believe this but she did want to meet the Wise One right away. "If he can foresee the future, I will find out if I will ever learn the secret of flying!" Penny thought excitedly. "Please take me to meet him," said Penny out loud.

A small group of penguins led Penny to a little hut made of sticks. The hut was open on one side and Penny saw the oldest looking penguin she had ever seen. "Why, his feathers are all gray instead of black," she observed. Penny also wondered about the pieces of glass she saw resting on his beak. You see, the Wise One's eyes were failing and he had to wear glasses.

"Come closer, Penny, so that I may see you better," the Wise One commanded. "Ah, yes, you are the one I see in my visions from time to time. Now what would you like to ask me?"

"Oh, Wise One, I wish to fly like the birds over the sea. When, if ever, will this happen to me?" Penny asked. "My dear, maybe you should be a poet instead of a pilot!" answered the Wise One as the other penguins giggled at Penny's rhyme. Not to be outdone, he also said, "Let me gaze into my crystal ball, and soon I will be able to tell you all!"

And with that, the Wise One waved his flippers over the glass ball in front of him. Then he chanted,

HENNO PECKTO SCANNO HIGH

WILL OUR PENNY EVER FLY?

Soon the cloudy ball began to clear. All the penguins gasped in amazement at the sight in the ball. There were penguins flying everywhere! Each penguin had on goggles and a shirt with lettering on the front. Just before the scene faded, Penny saw a barn on the ground. It had big letters painted on the roof.

GAL FLIGHT SCHOOL

The ball became cloudy once again. "This is all we shall see for today. It took all my energy to get that picture for you," said the Wise One as he waved them away and closed his eyes.

"Oh, boy! I know where I am going! Can you imagine that? A flight school for penguins just like me! Now all I have to do is find out what GAL stands for! Gosh, maybe it means a flight school only for girls."

Penny was so excited she clapped her flippers together. All this noise made Penny open her eyes. Where were all the penguins? And what was she doing on a boat? "Oh, silly me, I have been dreaming all this time. And here I thought I had another adventure where penguins were actually flying."

When Penny got up and waddled over to the side of the boat, she did notice something strange.

Instead of seeing GOOD HOPE on its side, she now saw the words CAPE HORN. "Maybe it would be a good idea to remember the letters GAL after all," thought Penny.

PENNY'S FIFTH ADVENTURE

Just when she thought she could take no more of life on the boat, Penny thought of a plan. Not a plan for escape, but a plan to relieve the boredom of the endless pattern of day and night. She had considered escape, but quickly gave up on the idea. "What am I going to do—jump off this boat in the middle of the ocean? Who knows? There might be a killer whale or leopard seal somewhere out there," Penny shuddered at this thought.

With all the eating and sleeping she was doing, Penny had become quite fat. "If I don't get some exercise soon, I will never learn to fly. I am getting so round, I may have to get a job as a beach ball!" Penny had seen some small children playing with these balls on Prince Phillip Island. The thought of being rolled back and forth over the sand made Penny giggle. She put one of her flippers over her beak to keep her laugh from being heard. "Oh, oh! Here come some humans," Penny cried. Two men were heading straight for Penny! Maybe they hadn't heard her. But one of the men carried a rope and Penny was sure it would be used to tie her up.

"Watch this, you old bloke. I'll show you how to get in shape!" one of the men said. Penny watched in amazement as the men took an end of the rope in each hand and began to swing it over his head. "I can't wait to see him trip and fall when it gets caught around his feet! I better not laugh out loud," Penny said to herself. But the man never fell. Every time the rope came near his feet, he jumped over it. Penny soon grew tired of watching this man and turned her attention to the other one.

"Now isn't this a strange sight! This man pushes himself up and down, up and down… He must be trying to see how long his nose is," Penny thought. Soon the men looked very wet. She peeked out from behind the barrel where she had stayed hidden from sight. She held out her flipper to see if it was raining. "Hmmm…It's not raining. I wonder why those men have drops of water on their faces?" mused Penny as she looked up at a clear blue sky. "Now don't you feel a lot better, mate?" said one man to the other. "You betcha! Why life on this ship would turn anyone into a slug!" the other replied. Penny had seen slugs on the beaches. A slug is like a snail, but does not have a shell. "Why that is what I feel like—a slug! I will try what those humans were doing."

Penny laid down flat on her belly and tried to push herself up using her flippers. She couldn't even lift herself one inch! "No wonder I cannot fly. My flippers are not strong enough to lift one feather. I better try that rope thing," thought Penny. Penny waddled over to one of the nets the men used for fishing. She used her beak to saw off a piece of the rope. She made a loop on each end and put each loop over her flippers. She swung the rope over her head and …WHAM! Penny had jumped too soon and the rope was now tangled at her feet. And to make matters worse, she had fallen flat on her face. "OUCH!" she cried, "I think I have broken my beak." Gingerly, she picked herself up and tried again. This time she tried to jump the rope using one foot at a time. It worked much better. "Hey! I am pretty good at this," smiled Penny, "This rope jumping will help me get stronger for flying."

Just then Penny heard shouts of "Land ahead! Land ahead!!" She rushed over to the edge of the boat. Sure enough, there was a large bay of water with land all around it. The thought of finally getting off the boat made Penny very excited. Then she heard the men arguing. "I told you we were on the wrong heading! Now we are way north of the Cape! One man yelled. "Aw, shut up! You couldn't read a compass well enough to find the bathroom in your own house." replied the other. "Well, you better get this ship out of the bay before we run aground," said another. When Penny heard this, she knew she could not spend another day on this deck. As the men turned and walked to the bow, Penny ran to the side and jumped. KERSPLASH!

Penny was thrilled to be in the water again. "My flippers didn't seem very strong on the boat, but look at me now!" she said. Suddenly Penny felt as though she was not alone. She looked behind her and there IT was. A whole group of animals with striped faces heading straight for her! She swam faster and faster, just staying beyond their reach. In a little bit, she felt the land beneath her feet and quickly scrambled onto the beach. "Whew! That was a close call!" gasped Penny, closing her eyes. She was exhausted. With her eyes closed, she did not see the stripe-faced animals scrambling onto the beach also. When Penny opened her eyes, they had her surrounded.

"Ark! Ark! Don't hurt me!" pleaded Penny. One of the animals stepped forward. "We won't hurt you. In fact, no one gets hurt here. This is the Golfo San Jose Marine Park. We are all protected by law," it said. As Penny looked at the group, her eyes became wide with surprise. Why these stripe-faced animals were penguins!

"Where am I?" asked Penny, "And what kind of penguins are you?" "We are the Magellanic penguins. We were named after a famous explorer that came to South America. You are actually in Argentina. Where did you come from?" they asked in return. "Oh, my goodness, I don't know where to begin. I am from Antarctica, but I was just in New Zealand, Australia, and Africa. Well, I guess I should say I visited Africa in a dream."

"Why do you travel so much, Penny?" the penguins asked, "You should settle down and have a family." "Oh, I have important things to do first. You see, I want to learn to fly!" Penny retorted. The Magellanic penguins looked at one another and rolled their eyes. "Penguins can't fly!" they chorused. "Oh, yes they can! I saw some doing it at a place called GAL FLIGHT SCHOOL. I intend to find out where that is, too!" cried Penny.

All the striped-faced penguins put their heads together and whispered amongst themselves. After their conference, they looked at Penny and shook their heads sadly. Then they began to walk away. "No wonder they dumped her off that boat- - the bird is crazy," a few of the penguins were heard to murmur. "Hey! Where is everybody going?" Penny asked, "Did I say something wrong?" She watched them all scurrying away. All, that is, except one penguin who motioned for Penny to follow him.

"PSST! PSST! Come over here behind this bush." He said. "They think you are loony," said this penguin. He saw the hurt look in Penny's eyes and quickly added, "But I know where your flight school is." Penny stared at this penguin in astonishment.

"You do? Tell me! Where is it? How do I get there?
And how do you know about it?" she asked. "Hold on,
hold on. One question at a time," he laughed. "I
didn't want to say anything in front of the others. You
saw how they acted. They never believe anything I
say. They think I am a dreamer. Anyway, the GAL
stands for Galapagos. They are a group of islands off
the coast of Ecuador." "Ecuador! What is that?"
demanded Penny. "It is a country on the northwest
side of South America," the penguin replied. "So, how
do I get to these islands?" asked Penny. "About the
only way there would be to fly," offered the penguin.
"FLY? I can't fly. That is why I want to go there," said
Penny.

"No, silly, you take an airplane. Have you ever
seen one?" asked her new friend. "Seen one? I have
been in two of them!" boasted Penny. "Oh boy! Now
that is what I always wanted. A ride in an airplane
would make my life complete. By the way, my name
is Paddy. What is your name?" he asked. "My name
is Penny. You still have not answered my last
question, Paddy. How do you know of this flight
school?" Penny asked.

"Well, one day I overheard two rheas talking," Paddy began to explain. "Rheas, what are those?" asked Penny. "A rhea is a large bird that looks like an ostrich," Paddy answered. "An ostrich? What is that?" Penny broke in. "It's a large bird that lives in Africa. Now stop with the questions for a minute, will you?" Paddy said. "I'm sorry to keep interrupting, but I want to know about these things." Penny replied.

"It is good to ask questions, but we have a saying here, Penny. CURIOSITY KILLED THE PENGUIN." Paddy warned. Penny thought she had heard this before. Why one of the humans had said it! But she didn't remember them saying it about a penguin. "Oh, well, I better shut up," Penny thought.

"Anyway, these two rheas were talking about how they wished they could fly. Those dumb rheas! Their wings are useless. They can barely jump off the ground, their bodies are so big. But they had a friend who just would not quit. He is the one who has been to the flight school on the Galapagos," Paddy explained.

Penny could not resist asking another question, "Well, did he do it? Did the rhea learn to fly?" Paddy shook his head, "I don't think so. You see the other two were laughing, because they had beaten him in the Annual Rhea Road Race. The one who had been to flight school had a terrible limp and could not run very fast. I heard he had an accident there and had to come home. And he sure didn't fly home by himself."

"Gee, that is too bad, "said Penny sadly, "But I am going to be very careful when I learn to fly. I am going to study all about it first. Now, how am I going to get to the Galapagos, Paddy?" Paddy looked up and said, "What do you mean, Penny? How are we going to get there? I am going with you!" Penny squealed with delight. "Oh, goody! It will be lots more fun having a friend along. But won't you miss all your other friends?" Paddy shook his head and replied, "I never did fit in with this crowd. After I told them that I wanted to ride in an airplane, they were not very friendly. But if you don't give it a try, you'll never fly! Right, Penny?" "Righto, Paddy! Let's go for it!" said Penny as she gave Paddy a "high flipper". (That is a penguins' way of giving a "high five", the way we do.)

Paddy motioned for Penny to come near him. He began to whisper, "Now, Penny, here is my plan.

Many times humans come here to see us. I have heard some of them say, 'When we get to the Galapagos, the animals will be much more friendly.' That means the humans must be going there. So we will follow the next group that says this and BINGO! We will be on the next flight to GAL FLIGHT SCHOOL. But first let's have a swim and a good meal." And with that, Penny and Paddy linked flippers and waddled happily to the ocean.

PENNY'S FINAL ADVENTURE

Penny and Paddy clambered up onto the beach after their swim. They began to make the plan that would get them to the Galapagos Islands.

"I'm telling you, Penny, all we have to do is wait for one of those tourist airplanes," said Paddy. "And then what, Paddy? We just get in line with all the humans and walk right into the plane? NOT! They won't allow it!" said Penny. "I suppose you are right," agreed Paddy, "We'll have to sneak into the cargo hold somehow. Let's go to the airport and see if we get any bright ideas there."

At the airport Paddy and Penny decided to watch the cargo planes instead of the passenger planes. All of a sudden Paddy elbowed Penny with his flipper. "PSSSSST! Penny, look over there!" They saw hundreds of boxes being put onto a plane. Each box had GAL. IS. stamped on it. Penny shouted with glee, "That's it! Those are the same letters I saw in the crystal ball. We have to get on that pane. But how?"

What Paddy and Penny needed at that moment was a distraction. Luckily for them, it happened. A sudden gust of wind came. "My hat! My hat!" cried a pretty young woman as her hat blew off her head. "I'll get it," said the man loading the boxes. He chased the hat down and gave it to the woman saying, "Aqui esta, senorita." "Gracias, senor," she replied.

"Here's our chance!" said Paddy as he pushed Penny toward the plane, "Let's go!" Together they waddled for it. They used the boxes as steps and finally hopped into the plane. It was perfect timing.

The man came back and loaded the final boxes, and then slammed the cargo door shut.

"I can't see! I can't see a thing!" yelled Paddy as he waddled around the boxes frantically. "Settle down, Paddy! OOPS! You ran right into me!" said Penny as she tried to calm him. "Gee, it doesn't get this dark at night," mumbled Paddy, "Guess I panicked for a moment there." "Just remember that this is the plane ride you've been waiting for," said Penny as she tried to take her mind off the darkness. She remembered her first time in the cargo hold and how afraid she had been. It all seemed so long ago. Would she ever get home again?

A loud noise made them jump! VAROOM! VAROOM! It was the engines running. The plane lurched forward and began to pick up speed. Penny wished she could see Paddy's face but it was too dark. She could hear him breathing in short gasps. "Holy mackerel! This thing is really moving! Never thought I'd live to see this day!" yelled Paddy.

When they lifted off the ground, Paddy shrieked, "I'm floating! I'm floating!" Penny chuckled and said, "Now can you see why I dream of flying?

And with just me up in the air, there wouldn't be all this noise." Paddy said, "This is my dream right here. What a feeling! I'd like to be able to see out of this thing. I wonder what all the penguins on the ground look like now. You know, Penny, I could probably peck a hole right through the floor with my beak. Then we would have a nice window." Before Penny could stop him, Paddy began to peck at the floor. PECK! PECK! PECKETY, PECK, PECK! "Ouch! Ouch!" cried Paddy, "This plane must be made of something other than dirt." Penny spoke up, "Why, Paddy, if you had pecked a hole in this plane, we would have fallen right out. Didn't you tell me that curiosity killed the penguin?" "So I did," replied Paddy, "Guess I'll have to wait until my next flight to look outside. I'm ready for a nap anyway. This has stressed me out." "Me, too" agreed Penny. And so the two penguins closed their eyes and slept the journey away.

Paddy and Penny awakened to find themselves sliding forward. "Hey! What is this?" asked Paddy. "We're landing!" said Penny, "We must be there! YIPPEE!" The plane coasted to a stop. Suddenly Paddy said, "How are we going to get off this thing?" Penny said, "Let's hide in the corner until all the boxes are taken off. Then we'll jump out." The cargo door opened and two men began unloading the boxes. "Hey, Mack, let's do half of these and take a break. I'm starving," one man said. "OK by me," said the other. They sat in the shade near the plane while they ate their sandwiches. "Sure is a gorgeous day here on Santa Cruz," one said as he stared out at the water. The other man happened to glance over at the plane and saw Penny and Paddy in the open doorway. "Hey! You dumb birds! Get outta there!" he yelled. They ran over to the plane just as Penny and Paddy dove out. "Can you believe that? Those penguins will get into just about anything. Why, they are even more curious than a cat. And everyone knows the saying, 'curiosity killed the cat'." The man said.

Penny looked at Paddy and said, "Did you hear that man. Paddy? He said curiosity killed the <u>cat</u>!! You told me a fib!" Paddy turned red and said, "Well, I must have gotten it mixed up." Penny glanced around and said, "Now I am the one who is mixed up. How are we going to find the flight school?" "Gee, I thought we would just look up and see a bunch of penguins flying in the sky," replied Paddy. "I certainly don't see any. So what is next? I guess we will just have to waddle around this island until we find it." And then they waddled and waddled and waddled and waddled...

Finally, Penny whined, "I'm hungry." Since they were near the ocean, they dove right into the water. The Humboldt current keeps the waters around the Galapagos Islands nice and cold. The two penguins snacked on some fish. They were so busy eating they didn't notice how far they were swimming. When they climbed out of the water, they were on a different island. What a sight greeted them. It was like a dream. There were hundreds of penguins everywhere! Some were even floating above the ground. They had huge triangles over them. Another penguin had what looked like an umbrella over it.

Another group of penguins was in a basket with a balloon overhead. Penny and Paddy just stared and stared. How did they all just float around up there?

In the meantime, an older penguin had waddled up to Penny and Paddy. He put out his flipper and said, "Welcome to San Christobal, you two. My name is Paulo." Penny could not believe her eyes. This was the penguin that the Wise One had seen standing next to the building with GAL FLIGHT SCHOOL written on it. Penny shrieked, "You're the penguin I say in the crystal ball! You are the one!" The older penguin looked strangely at Penny and spoke, "Now I never saw you before. And this island's name is San Christobal not Crystal Ball. Where did you two come from anyway?"

Paddy spoke first, "We came from Patagonia country in Argentina." Paulo replied, "No kidding! I had a sister who mover there. She nearly died there, too. Have you ever seen one of those humans drinking out of a metal can? The humans buy them in groups of six with little plastic rings around each can. She got her neck caught in one of those and it nearly strangled her. Sure wish those humans would take their trash with them." Paddy agreed, "Yes, this earth would be a better place if humans would clean up after themselves. Have you ever seen places where humans have never been? They're beautiful and the air smells so nice. But enough about humans, Paulo. What do you do here?"

Paulo said proudly, "I am the teacher for the flight school. Here we give birds who can't fly the chance to try it." Penny was hopping up and down. "Oh boy, oh boy, oh boy! Sign me up right now. When can I get in the air with those other birds?" Paulo grinned and said, "I appreciate your enthusiasm, Penny. But before we let you loose up there, you must complete ground school." "Ground school?" snorted Penny. "I know all about the ground. Spent my whole life there! I want to get off the ground." Paulo replied, "Safety first, Penny. Unless you understand the basic principles of flight you could have a serious accident. And I'm proud to say that has never happened here."

"Alright, so when do I start this ground school?" Penny asked. "Tomorrow morning...6:00 a.m. sharp. See you then. Will you be joining us too, Paddy?" "Nope. I'm, here strictly as a spectator. I already had my wish granted...a ride on an airplane." Paddy said.

Penny was so excited that she hardly slept a wink that night. "My dream has come true, my dream has come true, my dream has come true," she kept saying over and over.

The next morning, Penny found herself sitting at a desk. There were four other penguins in the same room. Soon Paulo waddled in. He looked more like a teacher with his glasses. "And now, class, you will learn the basics of flying. After one week of ground school, you will be ready to test your knowledge in the air," Paulo began. All the penguins glanced at one another. They all had a look of bliss on their faces. "Why, flying must be their dream, too," thought Penny. It had never occurred to her that other penguins might want to do the same thing. Every penguin she had met thought the very idea was silly.

"Penny, what is the most important part of anything that flies?" Penny's attention quickly snapped back to Paulo's question. "Well, sir, if I were to fly, the most important part would be my flippers. But you know I tried to fly once and they didn't seem to work very well. I ended up with a very sore beak." The other penguins snickered as Paulo answered, "You are actually correct, Penny. The most important part of a flying machine is the wing. And that is why you didn't do so well. The flippers of a penguin have changed over the years. They are no longer good for flying. So how could you fly? At GAL FLIGHT SCHOOL, we will have to make an artificial wing for you. And now I must ask you to make a decision. Some of you may wish to merely float through the air. In that case, a parachute or hot air balloon will do the trick. However, the closest we can come to flying will require something a little more daring. This is the thrill of hang gliding. I will not mislead you, though. This is a very dangerous sport unless you have the proper guidance. Please raise your flipper if you wish to hang glide." To her surprise, only Penny and another penguin named Pete raised a flipper.

"O.K. Penny and Pete will stay with me. The rest of you will report to Hanger #2." Penny and Pete eagerly learned all they could about hang gliding. They learned about the takeoff, soaring, and finally how to land. Words such as lift, drag, pitching and stall were used every day. Pete's ears perked up when Paulo used the word 'pitching' to describe how a wing will tuck its edge only to plunge downward. "And I thought pitching was what we did when we played baseball," he said. Penny's eyebrows shot up. "Baseball? What is that?" she asked. "Why, it's our national pastime in the United States. You hit a ball with a stick. It's great fun, if you can waddle around the bases pretty fast. Everyone in my town played it. I come from Chicago. Did I have fun sneaking out of that zoo! I sure showed those humans a thing or two. Ha! Ha!" laughed Pete. Penny couldn't resist asking, "What is a zoo?" Pete explained, "It's a place where different kinds of animals are kept in boxes and humans come to look at them."

"Boxes! You mean you have to live in a box? How awful. Are there windows in the boxes? I think I would die if I had to live like that." whined Penny. Pete said, "It's actually an open box surrounded by bars. You do get a good meal every day. And you don't have to fish for it. But it gets to be quite boring seeing all those humans day after day. They make noises and funny faces at us. But they all have to go home at a certain time, so we do get some relief from them."

"Hey! Are you two here to learn about flying, or do you just want to visit with each other?" yelled Paulo. Both Penny and Pete quickly shut their beaks and gave the teacher their full attention. To their delight, Paulo announced, "I do believe you are ready for your first flight. Get a good nights' rest and I'll see you in the morning."

Once again, Penny could hardly get to sleep. But she knew she must be well rested in order to fly. "I'll just try that trick that Mom taught me when I was a baby. I'll count krill. One, two, three, four, five…" With visions of herself in the air, she soon fell asleep.

Penny was awakened by Pete's voice, "Rise and shine! We're soon going to be doing a little rising ourselves!" Penny giggled and raced Pete to breakfast. Then they ran to Hangar #1. They were greeted by Paulo, who laughed and said, "Slow down, you two. You are going to need all that energy to help carry your kites up that hill. Did you know it is your lucky day? The wind is blowing straight up the hill. You will have perfect launch conditions. Let's go."

Penny and Pete trudged up the hill. They each carried their own glider by balancing the control bar on their shoulders. Pete glanced at Penny and said, "Did you ever think flying would be so much work? All those seagulls I watched never had to do this." Penny was so tired, all she could do was nod her head. Once they got to the top of the hill, they took a rest.

Paulo used this time to give a few last minute instructions. "Now remember to waddle as fast as you can, straight into the wind. Try not to drop the wing on either side or you may do a ground loop." Pete cut in, "I plan on doing my loops in the air, Paulo." To which Paulo replied, "Oh no you don't. Today we are just practicing the basics. You can become a stunt penguin on your own. Now the next step is to gently push the control bar forward. This will lift the nose and you will be off! Don't push too much or the glider will stall and you'll be back on the ground. Once you are in the air, pull the bar back. The nose will come down and you will pick up flying speed. Ready to go?" "YES!" cried Penny and Pete as they 'high-flippered' one another.

"Ladies first," said Pete as he winked at Penny. She took a deep breath and began to waddle as fast as she could. She pushed the bar out as she reached the edge of the hill. The wind pushed against the kite and it became taut. Penny realized she had lifted off the ground! "Oh, my!" screamed Penny, "I'm flying! I'm flying! Hey, what's happening?" She heard Paulo yelling instructions, "Pull back Penny, you are stalling!" Penny corrected the control bar just in time and picked up her air speed. "Whew! That was a close call," she thought with relief.

Penny looked down and could not believe her eyes. Everything looked so different from up above. "Gee, all those penguins look like ants from up here. One of those ants is waving at me!" Sure enough, it was Paddy. "That girl is really flying high," he said to himself. In fact, Penny was "soaring". She was able to do this, because of the ridges along San Christobal's coastline. The wind hit the ridge and went up, taking Penny with it.

Penny was now flying toward the water. "Oh, oh. I better turn so I don't fall into the water. I'm not sure I could swim with this thing," Penny murmured. She was right. To keep herself aloft, Penny had to stay near the ridge's air currents. Remembering what Paulo had said, "Just push your body in the direction you want to go." Penny pushed her body to the right. Immediately, the kite began to turn. "This is amazing!" thought Penny. "Everything works just like Paulo taught us. Thank goodness for ground school."

As Penny moved away from the ridges, she began to lose altitude. She spotted the landing area and turned toward it. Slowly, slowly, slowly she began to go down. She turned into the wind again and pushed the bar forward gently. When she was just a few inches off the ground, she pushed the bar forward and was in a full stall landing. She put her feet down and ran with the kite for a bit. She had done it!

Penny disconnected from the glider and hopped up and down. "I did it! I flew! I am a real bird now!" she shrieked. Paulo and Pete watched her and laughed. The Paulo turned to Pete and said, "Your turn!" Pete ran quickly and launched his kite into the air. "I'll show Penny how it is done. I'm even going to remember to pull back now." And pull back Pete did. Only he did it too much. The kite was making a nosedive for the ground! Pete now pushed forward as far as he could. Now he was stalling. Pete fell to the ground, right on his behind. Penny and Paulo ran to him, "Are you all right, Pete?" Pete looked ashamed as he said, "My bottom hurts. But my pride is hurt even more. And I was really going to show off for Penny. Oh well, maybe next time." "You'll have lots of 'next times', Pete. Flying takes a lot of practice. Everyone makes a mistake now and then. Just be happy you didn't get hurt." Paulo said. "You are right, Paulo. It's just that Penny flew so far and so well, her very first time. How can you explain that?" asked Pete. "Sometimes a penguin can dream about something for a very long time. Pretty soon their dreams almost become real. Even though today was Penny's first time in the air, I have a hunch she had practiced hundreds of times before. And she was willing to take the biggest step of all. To try! So many penguins have dreams but they are often afraid to make an attempt to realize them. Remember:

THOSE WHO TRY QUITE OFTEN FLY!"

Later that evening, Penny and Pete waddled down by the water. Pete looked at Penny and said, "I sure admired your flying today, Penny. You know, you look as beautiful on the ground as you did in the air." Penny was speechless and all she could do was smile at Pete. "He must really like me," thought Penny. "Maybe someday we could both fly back to Antarctica. Wouldn't everyone be amazed?" She was so happy that she had finally found another penguin that shared her dream.   Pete put his flipper around Penny and hugged her to him as they watched the sunset.

Made in the USA
Columbia, SC
22 November 2024

47010651R00030